1935 if
read a good
either a lot of money or a library card.
Cheap paperbacks were available, but their
poor production generally mirrored the quality
between the covers. One weekend that year,
Allen Lane, Managing Director of The Bodley Head,
having spent the weekend visiting Agatha Christie,
found himself on a platform at Exeter station trying to
find something to read for his journey back to London.
He was appalled by the quality of the material he had to
choose from. Everything that Allen Lane achieved from that
day until his death in 1970 was based on a passionate belief
in the existence of 'a vast reading public for *intelligent*
books at a low price'. The result of his momentous vision
was the birth not only of Penguin, but of the 'paperback
revolution'. Quality writing became available for the price of
a packet of cigarettes, literature became a mass medium
for the first time, a nation of book-borrowers became a
nation of book-buyers – and the very concept of book
publishing was changed for ever. Those founding
principles – of quality and value, with an overarching
belief in the fundamental importance of reading –
have guided everything the company has
done since 1935. Sir Allen Lane's
pioneering spirit is still very much alive
at Penguin in 2005. Here's to
the next 70 years!

MORE THAN A BUSINESS

'We decided it was time to end the almost customary half-hearted manner in which cheap editions were produced – as though the only people who could possibly want cheap editions must belong to a lower order of intelligence. We, however, believed in the existence in this country of a vast reading public for intelligent books at a low price, and staked everything on it'
Sir Allen Lane, 1902–1970

'The Penguin Books are splendid value for sixpence, so splendid that if other publishers had any sense they would combine against them and suppress them'
George Orwell

'More than a business … a national cultural asset'
Guardian

'When you look at the whole Penguin achievement you know that it constitutes, in action, one of the more democratic successes of our recent social history'
Richard Hoggart

The Scales of Justice

JOHN MORTIMER

PENGUIN BOOKS

PENGUIN BOOKS

Published by the Penguin Group
Penguin Books Ltd, 80 Strand, London WC2R ORL, England
Penguin Group (USA) Inc., 375 Hudson Street, New York, New York 10014, USA
Penguin Group (Canada), 10 Alcorn Avenue, Toronto, Ontario, Canada M4V 3B2
(a division of Pearson Penguin Canada Inc.)
Penguin Ireland, 25 St Stephen's Green, Dublin 2, Ireland
(a division of Penguin Books Ltd)
Penguin Group (Australia), 250 Camberwell Road, Camberwell, Victoria 3124,
Australia (a division of Pearson Australia Group Pty Ltd)
Penguin Books India Pvt Ltd, 11 Community Centre,
Panchsheel Park, New Delhi – 110 017, India
Penguin Group (NZ), cnr Airborne and Rosedale Roads, Albany,
Auckland 1310, New Zealand (a division of Pearson New Zealand Ltd)
Penguin Books (South Africa) (Pty) Ltd, 24 Sturdee Avenue,
Rosebank 2196, South Africa

Penguin Books Ltd, Registered Offices: 80 Strand, London WC2R ORL, England

www.penguin.com

'A Part of Life', extracted from *Clinging to the Wreckage*,
first published by Weidenfeld & Nicolson 1982
'Rumpole and the Scales of Justice' first published,
in a longer version, by Viking 1998
This selection first published as a Pocket Penguin, 2005

1

Copyright © Advanpress, 1982, 1998
All rights reserved

The moral right of the author has been asserted

Set in 11/13pt Monotype Dante
Typeset by Palimpsest Book Production Limited
Polmont, Stirlingshire
Printed in England by Clays Ltd, St Ives plc

Contents

A Part of Life

'You want to be a writer?' my father said, after I had told him that I had sold my first short story to the *Harrovian* for ten bob. 'My dear boy, have some sort of consideration for your unfortunate wife. You'll be sitting around the house all day wearing a dressing-gown, brewing tea and stumped for words. You'll be far better off in the law. That's the great thing about the law, it gets you out of the house.'

The war, which had removed most of the young barristers, had done wonders for my father's practice. He rose, most days, in Court, fixed witnesses with his clear blue, sightless eyes and lured them into confessions of adultery, cruelty or wilful refusal to consummate their marriages. As soon as he could he caught the train back from London (no after Court conference with him was ever known to last more than twenty minutes) to the wonders of his garden. I don't know if I can describe it or whether it has become, during the years I have lived here, over-familiar, like faces you see every day.

In his twenty acres of chalky fields there were two inexplicable dells, great holes in the ground which long ago may have been burial-places, or gravel pits, and are now filled with beech trees. Near to them my father built a small thirties' house with white walls and green tiles, a building in the sort of Spanish musical-comedy tradition, handed down through the garages on the Great West Road, which pleased the architect he employed. It still has light-fittings which might have come from the Savoy Hotel. Away from the house he planned huge herbaceous borders to stretch away to a field of magnolias and rarer ornamental trees. In the spring the copses are full of daffodils and narcissi. Tall, pale green and white Japanese flowering cherries, which he planted, tremble in the twilight like enormous ghosts. He planned the large kitchen garden with fruit cages in which loganberries and white raspberries, gooseberries and melons and strawberries grew, usually in the company of some panic-stricken and imprisoned bird. It is a great feeding-place for marauders from the beech woods. Pheasants, jays and pigeons ravish the vegetables. Deer, which have gone back to nature after escaping from a nearby park, glide across the lawn in the misty mornings and eat the rose-buds. At night there is a great noise of owls, and in my father's day we often used to see glow-worms, although they seem rarer now.

As my father could see none of these splendours he got my mother to describe them to him and in the evenings he would dictate to her a log, a diary of the garden's activities which also contained glimpses, cursorily noted, of human endeavour. Turning the thick volumes, written out in my mother's clear art-school handwriting, I can find out exactly what went wrong with the peas in 1942 and how they coped with greenfly on the roses. It is harder to discover when I was married, had children, got divorced or called to the bar, although most of the facts are there some-where, stuck at the far end of the herbaceous border. 'A most miserable cold and wet May,' a typical entry reads. 'Laburnums are now at their best. Mrs Anthony Waterer and Lady Waterlow are the only roses in flower. All liquidambars appear to be dead, but remaining newly planted trees and shrubs are doing well. John left for Paris after taking his Real Property exam, which he failed.' Or, 'The cats have brought up two litters by stealth. Smith has planted out the wallflowers, staked the borders and started to clean the strawberry beds. The green woodpecker flew through the French windows while we were sitting here. Now the divorce is over John is to be married in August.'

The work in the garden, which had grown so out of proportion to the house it surrounded, was never-ending. My father sat on a wooden stool wearing a straw hat, groping for weeds and dead-heads, with my mother beside him keeping up a running commentary. We had a gardener called Mr Smith, who looked very much like the late King George VI, and a gardener's boy who got blamed for everything and sat behind the potting-shed reading *Titbits* and wrote 'The Garden of Eden' on all the plant labels.

I cannot discover that I did much gardening in those days. Not long after I met my first wife there is an entry which reads, 'On Christmas Eve John and I amused ourselves by digging a hole and planting the Eucryphia in it', but I think I must have been waiting anxiously for a letter or a telephone call, and turned to the entertaining hole for relief. There was one duty my father and I always shared, whenever I was available, and that was drowning the earwigs.

The ceremony of the earwigs, which became, in my father's garden, a cross between Trooping the Colour and a public execution, had its origins in my most distant childhood. My father was fond of big, highly-coloured and feathery dahlias, large as side-plates or ladies' hats, and these blooms were a prey to earwigs. I have no idea where my father learnt to fight these pests in the way he did, or in the macabre imagination of what tweedy gardening expert the plan was born. It suffices to say that it was a scheme of devilish cunning. Stakes were planted in the ground near the dahlias and on top of each stake hung an inverted flowerpot lined with straw. The gorged earwig, having feasted on the dahlia, would climb into the flowerpot for a peaceful nap in the straw, from which it was rudely awakened by my father and myself on our evening rounds. We would empty the flowerpots into a bucket of water. On a good foray we might drown up to a hundred earwigs, which my father would pronounce, with relish, to be a 'moderately satisfactory bag'.

The times I most clearly remember with my father were the long walks we took together when I would guide him through the dark, insect-buzzing woods, steering him past the tentacles of bramble, keeping him away from branches where the gamekeepers had gibbeted magpies and squirrels as a warning to others. We used to sit by the fire at night, he in the wing-chair I still use, massaging his sightless eyes, and I read him what I had begun to write, another novel about Henley, the town below us in the valley, the Brewery and the Regatta. Sometimes he would laugh at the jokes. Sometimes he said, 'Sorry stuff', or, 'Rather poor fooling', and I knew, furiously, that he was right.

I was an advocate, my father was both a fine advocate and a good lawyer. He understood the law and loved it and when it was at its most obscure, as in the doctrine of the 'renvoi' in the cases on domicile, or of 'dependent relative revocation' in Probate, he found it as enjoyable as budding roses or doing *The Times* crossword. To the courtroom advocate, who only needs a basic instinct about the rules of evidence and the ability to look things up, law is an unwelcome mystery which only appeals to academics or those who practise in the Chancery Division. To me the law seems like a sort of maze through which a client must be led to safety, a collection of reefs, rocks and under-water hazards through which he or she must be piloted. The basic morality on which law is founded has always seemed to me crudely inferior to those moral values which everyone must work out for them-selves; and the results of even the best laws, when consistently applied, are bound to be intolerable in many individual cases. Moreover the law exists when it is being lived through people's lives and in Courts. Looked at in a book, or belted out as a lecture, it can have only a theoretical interest and hold a tenuous grasp on the attention.

'I think we might run to Oxford,' my father had said, 'provided you fall in and read the law.' I still felt that my time was likely to be short and my future, as the news of the war grew more depressing, uncer-tain. In the meanwhile I fell in and read law with no real faith in ever surviving to practise it. Again I wondered about my father's choice. Why Oxford? He'd been at Cambridge and Brasenose was a college he'd only heard mentioned, in an apparently disparag-ing way, by someone in his Chambers many years before. But as he offered me Oxford like the sausages and scrambled eggs of the condemned man's break-fast, I felt it churlish to refuse.

Oxford, after the Fall of France, as the black-out was pinned up in the Buttery, as Frank Pakenham, not yet Lord Longford and then history tutor at Christ Church, was shot in the foot by a cook whilst drilling with the Home Guard in the Meadows, was at the end of an era and I was at the end of my extraordinary middle-class, thirties' education. I can't say that I came out of this bizarre hot-house and met the 'real world' at Oxford. That encounter, intoxicating, painful, invigorating, hilarious and tragic, was held from me until, in the company of GIs, cameramen, electricians, aircraft workers with their Veronica Lake hairdos tied up in head-scarves, continuity girls and prop-men, I stopped being educated and came, belatedly, to life. Meanwhile I lay becalmed at Oxford.

The Oxford of the twenties and thirties was still there, like college claret, but it was rationed, on coupons, and there was not very much of it left. The famous characters still behaved as though they lingered in the pages of *Decline and Fall*. They were famous for being nothing except Oxford characters; once they left their natural habitat in Magdalen or The House they grew faint and dim and ended up down back corridors in Bush House, or as announcers on Radio Monte Carlo. They had double-barrelled names like Edward Faith-Peterson and Tommy Motte-Smith. By day they lay naked in their rooms, listening to Puccini or to Verdi's *Requiem*. By night they would issue into the black-out, camel-hair coats slung across their shoulders, bow-ties from Hall Bros

settled under their lightly-powdered chins, to take the
exotic dinner (maximum spending allowed under the
Ministry of Food regulations five bob) at the smartest
restaurants. What did it matter if the omelette were
of dried egg or the drink rationed Algerian or even
black-market Communion wine topped up with spirits (Gin and Altars)? They still talked about Firbank
and Beardsley and how, sometime in the long vaca-
tion, they had met Brian Howard, supposed model
for an Evelyn Waugh character, itching in his 'A.C.
Plonk's' uniform in the downstairs bar at the Ritz.

The high life of Oxford was something I never
encountered when I first moved into my rooms in
Meadow Buildings. To my dismay I found I was shar-
ing them with Parsons, a tall man with bicycle-clips
and a pronounced Adam's apple, who tried to lure
me into the Bible Society. One night Oliver and I
boiled up Algerian wine, college sherry and a bottle
of Bols he had stolen from his mother's flat, in
Parsons' electric kettle. When I recovered from the
draught I found Parsons wearing cycle-clips and
kneeling over me in prayer. I also heard, coming
from down the corridor, the sound of Brahms's
Fourth Symphony like music from some remote
paradise.

In fact my memory of Oxford seems, looking back
over a vast distance, to consist almost entirely of
Brahms's Fourth Symphony, a piece of music of

which I have become decreasingly fond, as I have lost the taste for bow-ties, Balkan Sobranie cigarettes and sherry and Bols boiled up in an electric kettle. But that music came from someone who did affect my view of the world, and of whom I still think with gratitude and bewilderment when I remember his serene life and extraordinary death.

My father, to whom I owe so much, never told me the difference between right and wrong: now, I think that's why I remain so greatly in his debt. But Henry Winter, who slowly and with enormous care sharpened a thorn needle to play Brahms on his huge gramophone, became a kind of yardstick, not of taste, but of moral behaviour. He had no doubts whatever about war, he knew that killing people was wrong. He looked forward with amused calm to the call-up, the refusal to put on uniform, the arguments before the tribunals and the final consignment to Pentonville or the Fire Service. He read Classics, and read them in the way I read Isherwood or Julien Green. He would sit in a squeaking basket chair, smoking a pipe and giving me his version of chunks of Homer and Euripides which, up to then, I had been trained to regard as almost insoluble crossword puzzles or grammarians' equations with no recognizable human content. I was born of tone-deaf parents, and in the school songs had been instructed to open my mouth soundlessly so that no emergent discord might mar the occasion. Yet Winter slowly, painstakingly introduced me to music, and the pleasure I take in it now is due entirely to him.

Winter's rejection of violence, and what seemed to me the extraordinarily gentle firmness of his moral stance, was the result of no religious conviction. He was courageously sceptical, fearlessly agnostic, open and reasonable with none of the tormented Christianity of my ex-roommate. Parsons had applied for a transfer after the desecration of his electric kettle and left me in solitary possession of a huge Gothic sitting-room and a bedroom almost the size of the waiting-room at St Pancras Station, with a chipped wash-basin in which I kept a smoked salmon, caught by my Aunt Daisy in Devon in defiance of rationing.

I suppose Oxford's greatest gift is friendship, for which there is all the time in the world. After Oxford there are love affairs, marriages, working relationships, manipulations, lifelong enemies, but even then, in rationed, blacked-out Oxford, there were limitless hours for talking, drinking, staying up all night, going for walks with a friend. Winter and I were emerging from the chrysalis of schoolboy homosexuality. At first the girls we loved were tennis-playing virgins posed, like Proust's androgynous heroine, forever unobtainable against a background of trees in the park, and carrying rackets and string bags full of Slazengers. There is nothing like sexual frustration to give warmth to friendship, which flourishes in prisons, armies, on Arctic expeditions and did well in wartime Oxford. Winter and I became inseparable and when, as time went on, I began to do things without him I felt twinges of guilt about my infidelity.

I had more time for friendship as I found the legal syllabus enormously dull and spent as little time at it as possible. To fulfil the bargain with my father, I acquired a working knowledge of Roman Law and after a year I knew how to manumit a slave, adopt an elderly senator or contract a marriage by the cere-mony of 'brass and scales', skills which I have never found of great service in the Uxbridge Magistrates Court. Roman Law was taught us by a mountainous old man who drank a bottle of whisky a day and who had, like the Royal Family, changed his German name for an old English one. He peered at me through glasses thick as ginger-beer bottles, and was forever veering away from Justinian's views on Riparian ownership to Catullus's celebration of oral sex, a change of subject which I found extremely welcome. Returning to Oxford by train from a legal dinner in London, this ancient Latinist mistook the carriage door for the lavatory and stepped out into the black-out and on to the flying railway lines outside Didcot. After his death I gave up Roman Law.

Other subjects I found encased in a number of slim volumes with titles like *Tort in a Nutshell, Potted Real Property* and *All You Need to Know About Libel and Slander*. I read them listening to Winter's gramophone, or as we punted down the river and the ATS in the long grass whistled *You Are My Sunshine* or sang, 'Keep smiling throo, Just as you, Used to do, Till the good times come again one sunny day'. If these were not good times we were deceived by never having known anything better.

The time came when Winter was about to face the tribunal which was to test the genuineness of his conscience. There was a man called Charles Dimont, a journalist and a character of great eminence in the pacifist world, who was said to be able to give Winter a lesson in how best to put his reluctance to kill people to a bench of sceptical and safely patriotic magistrates. Winter told me that a favourite question was, 'What would you do if you saw a German raping your grandmother?' to which he intended to reply, 'Wait until he'd finished and then bury the dear old lady again.' We went by bus to Boar's Hill, where Charles Dimont lived. When we got to his cottage he had a bad cold and was wearing a dressing-gown. There seemed to be a large number of small children about, one of whom was dropping raspberry jam into *The Bible Designed To Be Read As Literature*. In the corner was a dark young woman of remarkable beauty who said nothing and looked as if she were heartily sick of the tramp of conchies through her sitting-room. Charles Dimont told Winter that it was very difficult to persuade the tribunal that you really didn't like killing people unless you believed in God.

He offered us a cup of tea, but the pot was empty and anyway we had to go.

As we waited for the bus I had no idea that Charles Dimont was about to change his mind and obtain an infantry commission. I had still less idea that in some distant peace I would marry the dark, silent Mrs Dimont and bring up her children. And I had no sort of hint of the extraordinary melodrama of violence in which Winter himself would die. I only knew that I was determined to avoid the heroism of the tribunals. I thought I would probably end up in the RAF ground staff.

No marriage I could possibly have contracted could have been more inconvenient from my father's point of view. He was the doyen of the Matrimonial Bar, and I couldn't marry Penelope Dimont without being dragged (as people used to say in those far-off days, when co-respondents were kept off the Queen's Lawn at Ascot lest they might scorch the turf) through the Divorce Courts. In addition she had four young daughters who menaced my father, to whom all visitors were unwelcome, with a mass invasion of ready-made grandchildren. Clearly he had to do something about these threats to his peace and security, and with the mixture of guile and effrontery with which he had managed to settle so many heavily-contested Probate actions, he chose to proceed, not by pointing out to me the dangers of marrying Penelope, but by persuading her that I was a hopeless proposition. He took her for a walk and told her that I had no money, few prospects and no sympathy for anyone who got ill. With her assets, a fine and attractive family, some bits and pieces of furniture and her own small car, he was quite sure that she could find better fish from a wider and richer sea.

Penelope's father was a Rector in the Cotswolds. It was in his grey-stone Rectory that I watched her dish out the huge lunches, the great roasts and mounds of vegetables, which her children consumed with wide-eyed determination. My future father-in-law was small and stout. He grew depressed after services, when he was troubled by the thought that he could no longer bring himself to believe any one of the Thirty-nine Articles. In time he gave up preaching sermons and took to showing short religious films in his church instead. I remember him stumping off wearing Wellington boots under his surplice to insulate himself against any electric shock provided by the projector. He ruined his health by smoking and eating too many heavy puddings, but I was always fond of the Rector and got on well with him. He told me that I should be hopelessly lost in my future marriage to Penelope unless I could 'keep a firm hand on her tiller'. Each of our fathers seemed to have hit on the same expedient, to play up the hopeless deficiencies in their own children's characters.

In a very short time my father grew fond of his family of ready-made grandchildren, and they had an easy access to him which I had never claimed at their ages. They climbed over him, felt in the waistcoat pocket where he kept mints and wine-gums for them, and blew on his gold watch causing it to fly miraculously open. They took at once to the garden I had seen built and then slowly discovered, and they cantered up to their knees in daffodils or rolled down into the copses. They showed no patience with the hunt for earwigs. My father's entry for 28 January 1948 ran: 'Today is mild and sunny. Smith has finished planting the rhododendrons and camellias against the hedge. John was called to the bar on Jan. 26th.'

There was no possibility of my marrying Penelope until she could get divorced, for which we had to supply evidence. We went, at ruinous expense, to several Brighton hotels but, on being questioned later, the staff quite failed to remember us. We went to even more expensive hotels and did our best, by burning holes in the sheets or screaming during the night, to make our visits memorable. We had no success, our appearance and personalities were clearly such that we created no impression. Finally we suggested a private detective. One afternoon we looked from the windows of the cottage we had then rented and saw a respectable-looking person in a bowler hat walking slowly up the front garden. He introduced himself as Mr Gilpin and we showed him up to our bedroom where he was delighted to find male and female clothing scattered.

In my first days at the bar I often saw Mr Gilpin in the Divorce Courts. He greeted me respectfully, but made no reference to his afternoon visit. Many years later he was engaged in an entirely justified action against the police, who had wrongfully and frivolously arrested him when he didn't get out of the way of a Panda car on a zebra crossing. Mr Gilpin needed a character witness for the purpose of these proceedings, and I was glad to be able to say that I had known the 'Private Eye' for many years and always had found him a person of the greatest respectability whose evidence had been, when I had occasion to test it, totally reliable.

Thanks to Mr Gilpin the divorce at last went through. 'August 27th, 1949,' my father dictated for the record. 'John and Penelope's wedding for which we cut all available flowers which Penelope arranged with great effect.' I had fled from the loneliness of my childhood into a large and welcoming family, but I was back where I began, in a flat in the Temple, playing with the children in Temple Gardens, and being looked after by my father's clerk.

The similarities between the bar and the stage have been frequently noticed, and if there has never been a more authoritative-looking judge than the actor, Felix Aylmer, there has never been a greater performer

on his day and in the right part than the criminal
defender, Sir Edward Marshall Hall. My father remembered Marshall Hall and it was not his classic
profile that he described to me, nor his flamboyant
oratory ('Look at her!' Sir Edward once said to a Jury,
pointing to his trembling client in the dock, a young
prostitute accused of murder. 'God never gave her a
chance. Will you?'). It was Marshall Hall's dramatic
entry into a courtroom that impressed my father. His
head clerk would come in carrying the brief and a
pile of white linen handkerchiefs, then came a second
clerk with the water carafe and an air-cushion
(lawyers and pilots, as a result of sitting for long
hours, are martyrs to piles). Sir Edward himself
would then burst through the swing-doors to be
installed in his place by a flurry of solicitors and
learned juniors. He would subside on to the inflated
rubber circle and listen to the case for the prosecution. If the evidence against Marshall Hall's client
looked black he would, so my father assured me,
slowly unfold the top handkerchief and blow, a clar-
ion call to battle. When the situation became desperate he would remove the air-cushion and reinflate it,
a process which always commanded the Jury's un-
divided attention.

There is no art more transient than that of the
advocate, and no life more curious. During his working days the advocate must drain away his own
personality and become the attractive receptacle for

the spirits of the various murderers, discontented wives or greedy litigants for whom he appears. His is the fine-drawn profile, the greying side-pieces, the richly-educated voice and knife-edged pin-striped trousers which everyone accused of crime allegedly wishes to possess. The advocate must acquire the art of being passionate with detachment and persuasive without belief. He must be most convincing when he is unconvinced. The advocate has this much in common with the religious mystic, he can only operate successfully when he is able to suspend his disbelief. Indeed belief, for the advocate, is something which is best kept in a permanent state of suspension. There is no lawyer so ineffectual as one who is passionately convinced of his client's innocence.

So, in growing into a way of life as a barrister who wrote, or, as I wanted to think of it, as a writer who did barristering, I was stretched between two opposite extremes. The writer cannot help exposing himself, however indecently. Every performance he gives, although cloaked in fiction, reveals his secret identity. And yet in the biography of Sir Edward Marshall Hall the great advocate's 'self' seems to have vanished. The props are there, the collection of revolvers and precious gems and the taste for rare claret; but the voices are those of the prisoners in the dock, such people as Robert Wood, the artist accused of the Camden Town Murder, and Madame Fahmy, who shot her husband in the Savoy Hotel.

They borrowed his personality to escape death and left him, as perhaps he always was, hollow. His life is merely their lives and nothing is left of Sir Edward but a list of 'Notable Trials' and a few anecdotes about his outrageous way with an air-cushion.

I suppose most barristers, even those condemned to a life in the Chancery Division, were once infected with a slight case of the 'Marshall Halls', just as the actor who has settled into an unambitious round of voice-overs for breakfast cereals once yearned to play Hamlet. I have never been able to go into a court-room without that twinge of excitement and dread which actors feel as they wait for their entrances and, although I have never owned an air-cushion, I was once accused of cracking Polo Mints loudly between my teeth to the distraction of the Jury. All advocates have their acting mannerisms. When I started off my career in defended divorce cases I greatly admired the smooth and elegant advocacy of Lord Salmon, who seemed to me to win his cases with all the noise and bluster of a perfectly-tuned Rolls-Royce coasting downhill. Cyril Salmon would take out his more valu-able possessions, his gold watch and chain, his heavy gold key-ring and cigarette-lighter and place them on the bench in front of him. Then he would plunge his hands deep into his trouser pockets and stroll negli-gently up and down the front bench lobbing fault-lessly accurate questions over his shoulder at the witness-box. Here, I thought, was a style to imitate.

For my early cross-examinations I would take off my battered Timex watch, lug out my bundle of keys held together with a piece of frayed string and pace up and down, firing off what I hoped were appropriate questions backwards. I continued with this technique until an unsympathetic Judge said, 'Do try and keep still, Mr Mortimer. It's like watching ping-pong.'

Rumpole and the Scales of Justice

'The Scales of Justice have tipped in the wrong direction. That's all I'm saying, Jenny. Now it's all in favour of the defence, and that makes our job so terribly hard. I mean, we catch the villains and, ten to one, they walk away from Court laughing.'

Bob Durden, resplendent in his Commander's uniform, appeared in the living-room of Froxbury Mansions in the Gloucester Road. He was in conversation with Jenny Turnbull, the hard-hitting and astute interviewer on the *Up to the Minute* programme.

'You've got to admit he's right, Rumpole.' She Who Must Be Obeyed could be as hard-hitting and astute as Jenny. 'Things have gone too far. It's all in favour of the defence.'

'You know who I blame, Jenny?' the Commander went on, 'I blame the lawyers. The "learned friends" in wigs. Are they part of the Justice System? Part of the Injustice System, if you want my honest opinion.' The Commander spoke from the television set, in a tone of amused contempt to which I took the greatest exception. 'It's all a game to them, isn't it? Get your guilty client off and collect a nice fat-cat fee from Legal Aid for your trouble.'

'Have you got any particular barrister in mind?' Jenny Turnbull clearly scented a story.

'Well, Jenny, I'm not naming names. But there are regular defenders down at the Old Bailey and they'll know who I mean. There was a case some time ago. Theft in the Underground. The villain, with a string of previous convictions, had the stolen wallet in his back-pack. Bang to rights, you might say. This old brief pulled a few defence tricks and the culprit walked free. We get to know them, "Counsel for the Devious Defence", and quite frankly there's very little we can do about them.'

'Absolute rubbish!' I shouted fruitlessly at the flickering image of the Commander.

'It's no good at all you shouting at him, Rumpole.' Hilda was painfully patient. 'He can't hear a word you're saying.' As usual, She Who Must Be Obeyed was maddeningly correct.

A considerable amount of time passed, and one memorable day, Ballard, the head of our Chambers, appeared in my room with a look of sublime satis-faction and the air of a born commander about to issue battle orders.

'This, Rumpole,' he told me, 'will probably be the most famous case of my career. The story, you'll have to admit, is quite sensational.'

'What's happened, Ballard?' I had no wish to fuel Soapy Sam's glowing self-satisfaction. 'What've you landed now? Another seven days before the rating tribunal?'

'I have been offered, Rumpole,' the man was blissfully unaware of any note of sarcasm; he was genuinely proud of his eventful days in Court with rateable values, 'the leading brief for the defence in *R. v. Durden*. It is, of course, tragic that a fine police officer should fall so low.'

Of course, I realized that the case called for a QC (Queer Customer is what I call them) and, as I have said, that the defendant policeman would never turn to Rumpole in a time of trouble. I couldn't help, however, feeling a momentary stab of jealousy at the thought of Ballard landing such a front-page, sensational cause célèbre.

'He hasn't fallen low yet.' I thought it right to remind our Head of Chambers of the elementary rules of our trade. 'And he won't until the Jury come back to Court and pronounce him guilty. It's your job to make sure they never do that.'

'I know, Rumpole.' Soapy Sam looked enormously brave. 'I realize I have taken on an almost superhuman task and a tremendous responsibility. But I've been able to do you a good turn.'

'What sort of good turn, exactly?' I was doubtful about Ballard's gifts, but then he told me.

'You see, the Commander went to a local solicitor, Henry Crozier – we were at university together – and Henry knew that Durden wouldn't want any flashy sort of clever-dick, defence QC. The sort he's spoken out against so effectively on the television.'

'You mean he picked you because you're not a clever dick?'

'Dependable, Rumpole. And, I flatter myself, trusted by the Courts. I persuaded Henry Crozier to give you the Junior brief. Naturally, in a case of this importance, I shall do most of it myself. If the chance arises you might be able to call some formal, undisputed evidence. And of course you'll take a note of my cross-examination.'

Soapy Sam was smiling at me in a way I found quite unendurable.

As I have said, Commander Durden's patch was an area not far from London, and certain important villains had moved into it when London's East End was no longer the crime capital. They ran chains of minicab firms, clubs and wine bars, they were shadowy figures behind Thai restaurants and garden centres. They dealt in hard drugs and protection rackets in what may have seemed, to a casual observer, to be the heart of Middle England. And no one could have been more Middle English than Doctor Petrus Wakefield, who carried on his practice in Chivering. This had once been a small market town with a broad main street, and had now had its heart ripped out to make way for a pedestrian precinct with a multistorey car park, identical shops and strict regulations against public meetings or yobbish behaviour.

Doctor Wakefield, I was to discover, was a pillar

of this community, tall, good-looking, in his fifties. He was a leading light in the Amateur Dramatic Society, chairman of various charities and the doting husband of Judy, pretty, blonde and twenty years his junior. Their two children, Simon and Sarah, were high achievers at a local private school. Nothing could have been more quietly successful, some might even say boring, than the Wakefields' lives up to the moment when, so it was alleged, Commander Bob Durden took out a contract on the doctor's life.

The local police force, as local forces did, relied on a body of informers, many of whom came with long strings of previous convictions attached to them, to keep them abreast of the crimes and misdemeanours which took place in this apparently prosperous and law-abiding community. According to my instructions, the use of police informers hadn't been entirely satisfactory. There was a suspicion that some officers had been using them to form relationships with local villains, to warn them of likely searches and arrests and to arrange, in the worst cases, for a share of the spoils.

Commander Bob Durden was commended in the local paper 'for the firm line he was taking and the investigation he was carrying out into the rumours of police corruption'. One of the informers involved was a certain Len 'the Silencer' Luxford, so called because of his old connections with quietened firearms, but who had, it seemed, retired from serious crime and started a window-cleaning business in Chivering. He was still able occasionally to pass on information, heard in pubs and clubs from his old associates, to the police.

According to Detective Inspector Mynot, Bob Durden met Len the Silencer in connection with his enquiry into police informers. Unusually, he saw Len alone and without any other officer being present. According to Len's statement, the Commander then offered him five thousand pounds to 'silence' Doctor Wakefield, half down and half on completion of the task, the choice of weapons being left to the Silencer. Instead of carrying out these fatal instructions, Len, who owed, he said, a debt of gratitude to the doctor for the way he'd treated Len's mother, warned his prospective victim, who reported the whole matter to Detective Inspector Mynot. The case might have been thought slender if Doctor Wakefield hadn't been able to produce a letter from the Commander he'd found in his wife's possession, telling Judy how blissfully happy they might be together if Petrus Wakefield vanished from the face of the earth.

Such were the facts which led to Bob Durden, who thought all Old Bailey defence hacks nothing but spanners in the smooth works of justice, employing me, as Ballard had made painfully clear, as his *junior* counsel.

*

'I'm afraid I have to ask you this. Did you write this letter to Doctor Wakefield's wife?'

'I wrote the letter, yes. She must have left it lying about somewhere.'

'You said you'd both be happy if Doctor Wakefield vanished from the face of the earth. Why did you want that?'

We were assembled in Ballard's room for a conference. The Commander, on bail and suspended from his duties on full pay, wearing a business suit, was looking smaller than in his full-dress appearance on the television screen. His solicitor, Mr Crozier, a local man and apparently Ballard's old university friend, had a vaguely religious appearance to go with his name; that is to say he had a warm smile, a crumpled grey suit and an expression of sadness at the sins of the world. His client's answer to my leader's question did absolutely nothing to cheer him up.

'You see, Mr Ballard, we were in love. You write silly things when you're in love, don't you?' The bark of authority we had heard on television was gone. The Commander's frown had been smoothed away. He spoke quietly, almost gently.

'And send silly e-mails to people who fancy you,' I hoped Soapy Sam might say, but of course he didn't. Instead he said, in his best Lawyers as Christians tone of deep solemnity, 'You, a married man, wrote like that to a married woman?'

'I'm afraid things like that do happen, Mr Ballard. Judy Wakefield's an extremely attractive woman.'

There had been a picture of her in the paper, a small, smiling mother of two who had, apparently, fallen in love with a policeman.

'And you, a police commander, wrote in that way to a doctor's wife?'

'I'm not particularly proud of how we behaved. But as I told you, we were crazy about each other. We just wanted to be together, that was all.'

Ballard apparently remained deeply shocked, so I ventured to ask a question.

'When you wrote that you'd both be much happier if he vanished from the face of the earth, you weren't suggesting the doctor would die. You simply meant that he'd get out of her life and leave you to each other. Wasn't that it?'

'Yes, of course.' The Commander looked grateful. 'You're putting it absolutely correctly.'

'That's all right. It's just a defence barrister's way of putting it,' I was glad to be able to say.

Soapy Sam, however, still looked displeased. 'You can be assured,' he told our client, 'that I shall be asking you the questions, Mr Durden. Mr Rumpole will be with me to take note of the evidence. I'm quite sure the Jury won't want to hear sordid details of your matrimonial infidelity. It won't do our case any good at all if we dwell on that aspect of the matter.'

Ballard was turning over his papers, preparing to venture on to another subject.

'If you don't mind my saying so,' I interrupted, I hoped not too rudely, 'I think the Commander's affair with the doctor's wife the most important factor in the case, whichever way you look at it. I think we need to know all we can about it.'

At this Ballard gave a thin, watery smile and once again bleated, 'As I said I shall be asking the questions in Court. Now, we can obviously attack the witness Luxford on the basis of his previous convictions, which include two charges of dishonesty. If you could just take us through your meeting with this man . . .'

'Did you use him much as an informer?' I interrupted, much to Ballard's annoyance.

But the Commander answered me, 'Hardly at all. In fact, I think it was a year or two since he'd given us anything. I thought he'd more or less retired. That was why I was surprised when he came to me with all that information about one of my officers.'

Durden then went through his conversation with the Silencer, which contained no reference to any proposed assassination. This was made quite clear in our instructions, so I excused myself and slipped out of the door, counted up to two hundred in my head and re-entered to tell Soapy Sam that our Director of Marketing and Administration wished to see him without delay on a matter of extreme urgency. Our leader excused himself, straightened his tie, patted down his hair and made for the door.

'Now then,' I gave our instructing solicitor some quick instructions as I settled myself in Ballard's chair, 'have a look at our client's bank statements, Mr Crozier. Make sure that an inexplicable two and a half thousand didn't get drawn out in cash. If the account's clean tell the prosecution you'll disclose it providing they give us the good Doctor's.'

'Very well, Mr Rumpole, but why . . . ?'

'Never mind about why for the moment. You might help me a bit more about Doctor Wakefield. I suppose he is pretty well known in the town. Has he practised there for years?'

'A good many years. I think he started off in London. A practice in the East End – Bethnal Green, that's what he told us. Apparently a pretty rough area. Then he came out to Chivering.'

'To get away from the East End?'

'I don't know. He always said he enjoyed working there.'

'I'm sure he did. One other thing. He is a pillar of the Dramatic Society, isn't he? What sort of parts does he play?'

'Oh, leads.' The solicitor seemed to brighten up considerably when he told me about it. 'The Chivering Mummers are rather ambitious, you know. We did a quite creditable *Othello* when it was the A-level play.'

'And the Doctor took the lead? You're not suggesting he blacked up? That's not allowed nowadays.'

'Oh, no. The *other* great part.'

'Of course.' I made a mental note. 'That's most interesting.'

A minute later, a flustered Ballard returned to the room and I moved politely out of his chair. He hadn't been able to find Luci with an 'i' anywhere in Chambers, a fact which came as no surprise to me at all.

When I got home to Froxbury Mansions, I happened to mention, over the shepherd's pie and cabbage, that Commander Bob Durden had admitted to an affair with the Doctor's attractive and much younger wife.

'That comes as no surprise to me at all,' Hilda told me. 'As soon as he appeared on the television I was sure there was something fishy about that man.'

I was glad to discover that, when it comes to telling lies, Hilda can do it as brazenly as any of my clients.

In the weeks before the trial, I thought a good deal about Doctor Petrus Wakefield. Petrus was, you will have to admit, a most unusual Christian name, perhaps bestowed by a pedantic Latin master and his classically educated wife on a child they didn't want to call anything as commonplace as Peter. What bothered me, when I first read the papers in *R. v. Durden*, was where and when I had heard it before. And then

I remembered old cases, forgotten crimes and gang rivalry in a part of London to the east of Ludgate Circus in the days when I was making something of a name for myself as a defender at the Criminal Bar. These thoughts led me to remember Bill 'Knuckles' Huckersley, a heavyweight part-time boxer, full-time bouncer, and general factotum of a minicab organization in Bethnal Green. I had done him some service, such as getting his father off a charge of attempting to smuggle breaking-out instruments into Pentonville while Bill was detained there. This unlooked-for success moved him to send me a Christmas card every year and, as I kept his latest among my trophies, I had his address.

I thought he would be more likely to confide in me than in some professional investigator such as the admirable Fig Newton. Accordingly, I forsook Pommeroy's one evening after Court and made instead for the Black Spot pub in the Bethnal Green Road. There I sat staring moodily into a pint of Guinness as a bank of slot machines whirred and flashed and loud music filled a room, encrusted with faded gilt, which had become known, since a famous shooting had occurred there in its historic past, as the Luger and Lime Bar.

Knuckles arrived dead on time, a large, broad-shouldered man who seemed to move as lightly as an inflated balloon across the bar to where I sat. He pulled up a stool beside me and said, 'Mr Rumpole!

This is an honour, sir. I told Dad you'd rang up for a meeting and he was over the moon about it. Eighty-nine now and still going. He sends his good wishes, of course.'

'Send him mine.' I bought Knuckles the Diet Coke and packet of curry-flavoured crisps he'd asked for and, as he crunched his way through them, the conversation turned to Doctor Petrus Wakefield. 'Petrus,' I reminded him. 'Not a name you'd forget. It seemed to turn up in a number of cases I did in my earlier years.'

'He treated friends of mine.' Knuckles lifted a fistful of crisps to his mouth and a sound emerged like an army marching through a field of dead bracken. 'They did get a few injuries in their line of business.'

'What do you mean by that, exactly?'

'Knife wounds. Bullet holes. Some of them I went around with used to attract those sort of complaints. You needed a doctor who wasn't going to get inquisitive.'

'And that was Doctor Petrus Wakefield?'

'He always gave you the first name, didn't he? Like he was proud of it. You got any further questions, Mr Rumpole? Don't they say that in Court?'

'Sometimes. Yes, I have. About Len Luxford. He used to come in here, didn't he?'

'The old Silencer? He certainly did. He's long gone, though. Got a window-cleaning business somewhere outside London.'

'Do you see him occasionally?'

'We keep in touch. Quite regular.'

'And he was a patient of Doctor Petrus?'

'We all were.'

'Anything else you can tell me about the Doctor?'

'Nothing much. Except that he was always on about acting. He wanted to get the boys in the nick into acting plays. I had it when I was in the Scrubs. He'd visit the place and start drama groups. I used to steer clear of them. Lot of dodgy blokes dressing up like females.'

'Did he ever try to teach Len Luxford acting?'

My source grinned, coughed, covered his mouth with a huge hand, gulped Diet Coke and said with a meaningful grin, 'Not till recently, I reckon.'

'You mean since they both lived at Chivering?'

'Something like that, yes. Last time I had a drink with Len he told me a bit about it.'

'What sort of acting are you talking about?' I tried not to show my feeling that my visit to the deafening Luger and Lime Bar was about to become a huge success, but Knuckles had a sudden attack of shyness.

'I can't tell you that, Mr Rumpole. I honestly can't remember.'

'Might you remember if we called you as a witness down the Old Bailey?'

My source was smiling as he answered, but for the first time since I'd known him his smile was seriously alarming. 'You try and get me as a witness down the Old Bailey and you'll never live to see me again. Not in this world you won't.'

After that I bought him another Diet Coke and then I left him. I'd got something out of Knuckles. Not very much, but something.

'This is one of those unhappy cases, Members of the Jury. One of those very rare cases when a member of the Police Force, in this case a very senior member of the Police Force, seems to have lost all his respect for the law and sets about to plot and plan an inexcusable and indeed a cruel crime.'

This was Marston Dawlish QC, a large, beefy man, much given to false smiles and unconvincing bonhomie, opening the case for the prosecution to an attentive Jury. On the Bench we had drawn the short straw in the person of the aptly named Mr Justice Graves. A pale, unsmiling figure with hollow cheeks and bony fingers, he sat with his eyes closed as though to shut out the painful vision of a dishonest senior copper.

'As I say, it is, happily, rare indeed to see a high-ranking police officer occupying that particular seat in an Old Bailey courtroom.' Here Marston Dawlish raised one of his ham-like hands and waved it in the general direction of the dock.

'A rotten apple.' The words came in a solemn, doom-laden voice from the Gravestone on the Bench.

'Indeed, your Lordship.' Marston Dawlish was only too ready to agree.

'We used to say that of police officers who might be less than honest, Members of the Jury.' The Judge started to explain his doom-laden pronouncement. 'We used to call them "rotten apples" who might infect the whole barrel if they weren't rooted out.'

'Ballard!' This came out as a stentorian whisper at my leader's back. 'Aren't you going to point out that was an appalling thing for the Judge to say?'

'Quiet, Rumpole!' The Soapy Sam whisper was more controlled. 'I want to listen to the evidence.'

'We haven't got to the evidence yet. We haven't heard a word of evidence, but some sort of judicial decision seems to have come from the Bench. Get up on your hind legs and make a fuss about it!'

'Let me remind you, Rumpole, I'm leading counsel in this case. I make the decisions –'

'Mr Ballard!' Proceedings had been suspended while Soapy Sam and I discussed tactics. Now the old Gravestone interrupted us. 'Does your Junior wish to say something?'

'No, my Lord.' Ballard rose with a somewhat sickly smile. 'My Junior doesn't wish to say anything. If an objection has to be made, your Lordship can rely on me to make it.'

'I'm glad of that.' Graves let loose a small sigh of relief. 'I thought I saw Mr Rumpole growing restive.'

'I am restive, my Lord.' As Ballard sat down, I rose

up like a black cloud after sunshine. 'Your Lordship seemed to be inviting the Jury to think of my client as a "rotten apple", as your Lordship so delicately phrased it, before we have heard a word of evidence against him.'

'Rumpole, sit down.' Ballard seemed to be in a state of panic.

'I wasn't referring to your client in particular, Mr Rumpole. I was merely describing unsatisfactory police officers in general.'

It was, I thought, a remarkably lame excuse. 'My Lord,' I told him, 'there is only one police officer in the dock and he is completely innocent until he's proved guilty. He could reasonably object to any reference to "rotten apples" before this case has even begun.'

There was a heavy silence. I had turned to look at my client in the dock and I saw what I took to be a small, shadowy smile of gratitude. Ballard sat immobile, as though waiting for sentence of death to be pronounced against me.

'Members of the Jury,' Graves turned stiffly in the direction of the twelve honest citizens, 'you've heard what Mr Rumpole has to say and you will no doubt give it what weight you think fit.' There was a welcoming turn in the direction of the prosecution. 'Yes, Mr Marston Dawlish. Perhaps you may continue with your opening speech, now Mr Ballard's Junior has finished addressing the Court.'

Marston Dawlish finished his opening speech

without, I was pleased to notice, any further support from the learned Judge. Doctor Petrus Wakefield was the first witness and he gave, I had to admit, an impressive performance. He was a tall, still, slender man with greying sideburns, slightly hooded eyes and a chin raised to show his handsome profile to the best possible advantage. When he took the oath he held the Bible up high and projected in a way which must have delighted the elderly and hard of hearing in the audience attending the Chivering Mummers. He smiled at the Jury, took care not to speak faster than the movements of the Judge's pencil, and asked for no special sympathy as a betrayed husband and potential murder victim. If he wasn't a truthful witness he clearly knew how to play the part.

An Old Bailey conference room had been reserved for us at lunchtime, so we could discuss strategy and eat sandwiches. Ballard, after having done nothing very much all morning, was tucking into a prawn and mayo when he looked up and met an outraged stare from Commander Durden.

'What the hell was that Judge up to?'

'Gerald Graves?' Ballard tried to sound casually unconcerned. 'Bit of an offputting manner, I agree. But he's sound, very sound. Isn't he, Rumpole?'

'Sound?' I said. 'It's the sound of a distant foghorn on a damp night.' I didn't want to depress the

Commander, but he was depressed already, and distinctly angry.

'Whatever he sounds like, it seems he found me guilty in the first ten minutes.'

'You mean,' I couldn't help reminding the man of his denunciation of defence barristers, 'you found the Scales of Justice tipped towards the prosecution? I thought you said it was always the other way round.'

'I have to admit,' and the Commander spoke as though he meant it, 'I couldn't help admiring the way you stood up to this Judge, Mr Rumpole.'

'That was standing up to the Judge, was it?' I couldn't let the man get away with it. 'Not just another courtroom trick to get the Jury on our side and give the Scales of Justice a crafty shove?'

'I don't think we should discuss tactics in front of the client, Rumpole.' Soapy Sam was clearly feeling left out of the conversation. 'Although, I have to say, I don't think it was wise to attack the Judge at this stage of the case or indeed at all.' He'd got the last morsel of prawn and mayo sandwich on his chin and wiped it on a large white handkerchief before setting out to reassure the client. 'From now on, I shall be personally responsible for what is said in Court. As your leading counsel, I shall do my best to get back on better terms with Graves.'

'You mean,' the Commander looked distinctly cheated, 'he's going to get away with calling me a rotten apple?'

'I mean to concentrate our fire on this man Luxford. He's got a string of previous convictions.' Ballard did his best to look dangerous, but it wasn't a great performance.

'First of all, someone's got to cross-examine the good Doctor Petrus Wakefield,' I reminded him.

'I shall be doing that, Rumpole. And I intend to do it very shortly. We don't want to be seen attacking the man whose wife our client unfortunately –'

'Rogered.' I was getting tired of Ballard's circumlocutions.

'Misconducted himself.' Ballard lowered his voice, and his nose, into a paper cup of coffee. This was clearly part of the case on which Soapy Sam didn't wish to dwell.

'You'll have to go into the whole affair,' I told him. 'It's provided the motive for the crime.'

'The alleged victim's a deceived husband.' Ballard shook his head. 'The Jury are going to have a good deal of sympathy for the Doctor.'

'If you ask him the questions I've suggested, they may not have all that much sympathy. You got my list, did you?'

'I have read your list carefully, Rumpole,' my leader said, 'and quite frankly I don't think there's anything in it that it would be helpful to ask Doctor Wakefield.'

'It might be very helpful to the prosecution if you don't ask my questions.'

'I shall simply say "My client deeply regrets his unfortunate conduct with your wife" and sit down.'

'Well, Commander,' I said, 'you've got a barrister who's going to keep the scales tipped in what you said was the right direction.'

'Towards justice?' Bob Durden was trying to stick to his old convictions as a drowning man might to a straw.

'No,' I said. 'Towards a conviction. If it's the conviction of an innocent man, well, I suppose that's just bad luck and part of the system as you'd like it to work.'

Mr Crozier looked embarrassed and the Commander was seriously anxious as he burst out, 'Are you saying, Mr Rumpole, that the questions you want asked could get me off?'

'At least leave you in with a chance.' I was prepared to promise him that.

'I'm just one of those legal hacks you disapprove of,' I told him. 'I want you to walk out of Court laughing. I know that makes me a very dubious sort of lawyer, the kind you really hate, don't you, Commander Durden?'

In the silence that followed, our client looked round the room uncertainly. Then he made up his mind and barked out an order. 'I want Mr Rumpole's questions asked.'

'I told you,' Ballard put down his half-eaten sandwich, 'I'm in charge of this case and I don't intend to make any attack on the reputable Doctor whose wife you apparently seduced.'

'All right.' In spite of Ballard's assertion of his authority it was the Commander who was in charge. 'Then Mr Rumpole is going to have to ask the questions for you.'

I was sorry for Soapy Sam then, and I felt, I have to confess, a pang of guilt. He had behaved according to his fairly hopeless principles and could do no more. He rose to his feet, left his half-eaten sandwich to curl up on its plate, and spoke to his friend Mr Crozier who looked deeply embarrassed.

'Under the circumstances,' Ballard said, 'I must withdraw. My advice has not been taken and I must go. I can't say I expect a happy result for you, Commander, but I wish you well. I suppose you're not coming with me, Rumpole?'

As I say, I felt for the man, but I couldn't leave with him. Commander Durden had put his whole life in the hands of the sort of Old Bailey hack he had told the world could never be trusted not to pull a fast one.

'Doctor Wakefield, you're suggesting in this case that my client, Commander Durden, instigated a plan to kill you?'

'He did that, yes.'

'It wasn't a very successful plan, was it?'

'What do you mean?'

'Well, you're still here, aren't you? Alive and kicking.'

This got me a little stir of laughter from the Jury and a doom-laden warning from his Lordship.

'Mr Rumpole, for reasons which we need not go into here, your learned leader hasn't felt able to continue in this case.'

'Your Lordship is saying that he will be greatly missed?'

'I am saying no such thing. What I am saying is that I hope this defence will be conducted according to the high standard we have come to expect from Mr Ballard. Do I make myself clear?'

'Perfectly clear, my Lord. I'll do my best.' Here I was looking at the Jury. I didn't exactly wink, but I hoped they were prepared to join me in the anti-Graves society. 'Of course I can't promise anything.'

'Well, do your best, Mr Rumpole.' The old Gravestone half closed his eyes as though expecting to be shocked by my next question. I didn't disappoint him.

'Doctor Wakefield, were you bitterly angry when you discovered that your wife had been sleeping with Commander Durden?'

'Mr Rumpole!' The Graves eyes opened again, but with no friendly expression. 'I'm sure the Jury will assume that Doctor Wakefield had the normal feelings of a betrayed husband.'

43

'I quite agree, my Lord. But the evidence might be more valuable if it came from the witness and not from your Lordship.' Before Graves could utter again, I launched another question at the good Doctor. 'Did you consider divorce?'

'I thought about it, but Judy and I decided to try to keep the marriage together for the sake of the children.'

'An admirable decision, if I may say so.' And I decided to say so before the doleful Graves could stir himself to congratulate the witness. 'You've produced the letter you found in your wife's handbag. By the way, do you make a practice of searching your wife's bag?'

'Only after I'd become suspicious. I'd heard rumours.'

'I see. So you found this letter, in which the Commander said they might be happier if you vanished from the face of the earth. Did you take that as a threat to kill you?'

'When I heard about the plot, yes.'

'When you heard about it from Luxford?'

'Yes.'

'But not at the time you found the letter?'

'It occurred to me it might be a threat, but I didn't believe that Bob Durden would actually do anything.'

'You didn't believe that?'

'No. But I thought he meant he wanted me dead.'

'And it made you angry?'

'Very angry.'

'So I suppose you went straight round to the Commander's office, or his house, and confronted him with it.'

'No, I didn't do that.'

'You didn't do that?' I was looking at the Jury now, in considerable surprise, with a slight frown and raised eyebrows, an expression which I saw reflected in some of their faces.

'May I ask why you didn't confront my client with his outrageous letter?'

'I didn't want to add to the scandal. Judy and I were going to try to make a life together.'

'That answer,' the sepulchral Graves' voice was now almost silky, 'does you great credit, if I may say so, Doctor Wakefield.'

'What may not do you quite so much credit, Doctor,' I tried to put my case as politely as possible, 'is the revenge you decided to take on your wife's lover. This letter,' I had it in my hand now and held it up for the Jury to see, 'gave you the idea. The ingenious revenge you planned would cause Bob Durden, and not you, to vanish. Isn't that the truth of the matter?'

'Are you suggesting, Mr Rumpole,' the Judge over-acted his astonishment, 'that we've all got this case the wrong way round and that it was Doctor Wakefield who was planning to murder your client?'

'Not murder him, my Lord. However angry the

Doctor was, however deep his sense of humiliation, he stopped short of murder. No. What he planned for Mr Durden was a fate almost worse than death for a senior police officer. He planned to put him exactly where he is now, in the Old Bailey dock, faced with a most serious charge and with the prospect of a long term of confinement in prison.'

It was one of those rare moments in Court of absolute silence. The clerk sitting below the Judge stopped whispering into his telephone, no one came in or went out, opened a law book or sorted out their papers. The Jury looked startled at a new and extraordinary idea, everyone seemed to hold their breath, and I felt as though I had just dumped my money on an outside chance and the roulette wheel had started to spin.

'I really haven't the least idea what you mean.' Doctor Petrus Wakefield, in the witness box, looked amused rather than shaken, cheerfully tolerant at a barrister's desperate efforts to save his client, and perfectly capable of dealing with any question I might have the wit to ask.

Graves swooped to support the Doctor. 'Mr Rumpole, I presume you're going to explain that extraordinary suggestion.'

'Your Lordship's presumption is absolutely correct. I would invite your Lordship to listen carefully while I put my case to the witness. Doctor Wakefield,' I went on before Graves could summon his voice back from the depths, 'your case is that you learnt of the alleged plot to kill you when Luxford called to warn you. We haven't yet heard from Mr Luxford, but that's your story.'

'It's the truth.'

'Luxford warned you because he was grateful for the way you'd treated his mother?'

'That is so.'

'But you'd known Len Luxford, the Silencer as he was affectionately known by the regulars in the Black Spot in Bethnal Green, long before that, hadn't you?'

Doctor Wakefield took time to think. He must have thought of what the Silencer might say when he came to give evidence and he took a gamble on the truth. 'I had come across him. Yes.'

'Because you practised as a doctor in that part of London?'

'I did, yes.'

'And got to know quite a number of characters who lived on the windy side of the law?'

'It was my job to treat them medically. I didn't enquire into the way they lived their lives.'

'Of course, Doctor. Didn't some of your customers turn up having been stabbed, or with gunshot wounds?'

'They did, yes.' Once again the Doctor took a punt on the truth.

'So you treated them?'

'Yes. Just as you, Mr Rumpole, no doubt represented some of them in Court.'

It was a veritable hit, the Jury smiled, the Gravestone looked as though it was the first day of spring, and I had to beware of any temptation to underestimate the intelligence of Doctor Wakefield.

'Exactly so. And like me, you got to know some of them quite well. You got to know Luxford very well in those old days, didn't you?'

'He was a patient of mine.'

'You treated his wounds and kept quiet about them.'

'Probably.'

'Probably. So would it be right to say that you and the Silencer Luxford went back a long time, and he owed you a debt of gratitude?'

'Exactly!' The Doctor was pleased to agree. 'Which is why he told me about your client's plan to pay him to kill me.'

'I'm just coming to that. When you're not practising medicine, or patching up old gangsters, you spend a great deal of your time acting, don't you?'

'It's my great passion.' And here the Doctor's voice was projected and enriched. 'Acting can release us from ourselves. Call on us to create a new character.'

'Which is why you encouraged acting in prisons.'

'Exactly, Mr Rumpole! I'm glad you understand that, at least.'

There was a moment of rapport between myself and the witness, but I had to launch an attack which seemed, now that I was standing up in a crowded courtroom, like taking a jump in the dark off a very high cliff.

'I think you encouraged Len Luxford to act?'

'In the old days, when I did some work with prisoners, yes.'

'Oh, no, I mean quite recently. When you suggested he went for a chat with Commander Durden about police informers and came out acting the part of a contract killer.'

The Doctor's reaction was perfect: good-natured, half amused, completely unconcerned. 'I really have no idea what you're suggesting,' he said.

'Neither have I.' The learned Gravestone was delighted to join the queue of the mystified. 'Perhaps you'd be good enough to explain yourself, Mr Rumpole.'

'Certainly, my Lord.' I turned to the witness. 'It was finding the letter that gave you the idea, wasn't it? It could be used to support the idea that Commander Durden wanted you dead. You were going to get your revenge, not by killing him, nothing as brutally simple as that, but by getting him convicted of a conspiracy to murder you. By finishing his career, turning him into a criminal, landing him, the rotten apple in the barrel of decent coppers, in prison for a very long time indeed.'

'That is absolute nonsense.' The Doctor was as calm as ever, but I ploughed on, doing my best to sound more confident than I felt.

'All you needed was an actor for your small-cast play. So you got Len Luxford, who owed you for a number of favours, to act for you. All he had to do was to lie about what Commander Durden had said to him when he arranged a meeting, and you thought that and the letter would be enough.'

'It's an interesting idea, Mr Rumpole. But of course it's completely untrue.'

'You're an excellent actor, aren't you, Doctor?' I took it slowly now, looking at the Jury. 'Didn't you have a great success in the Shakespeare play you did with the local Mummers?'

'I think we all did fairly well. What's that got to do with it?'

'Didn't you play Iago? A man who ruins his Commander by producing false evidence?'

'Mr Rumpole!' Graves' patience, fragile as it was, had clearly snapped at what he saw as my attempt to call a dead dramatist into the witness box. 'Have you no other evidence for the very serious suggestions you're making to this witness except for the fact that he played, who was it?' He searched among his notes. 'The man Iago?'

'Oh yes, my Lord.' I tried to answer with more confidence than I felt. 'I'd like the Jury to have a couple of documents.'

Mr Crozier had done his work well. Having surrendered Bob Durden's bank statements to the young man from the Crown Prosecution Service, he seemed to take it for granted that we should get Doctor Wakefield's in return. Now the Judge and the Jury had their copies, and I introduced the subject.

'Let me just remind you. Luxford saw Commander Durden on March the fifteenth. On March the twenty-first you went to Detective Inspector Mynot with your complaint that my client had asked Luxford to kill you for a payment of five thousand pounds, two and a half thousand down and the balance when the deed was done.'

'That's the truth. It's what I told the Inspector.'

'You're sure it's the truth?'

'I am on my oath.'

'So you are.' I looked at the Jury. 'Perhaps you could look at your bank statement. Did you draw out two and a half thousand pounds in cash on March the twenty-first? Quite a large sum, wasn't it? May I suggest what it was for?'

For the first time the Doctor missed his cue, looked about the Court as though hoping for a prompt, and, not getting one, invented. 'I think I had to pay . . . I seem to remember . . . Things were done to the house.'

'It wasn't anything to do with the house, was it? You were paying Len Luxford off in cash. Not for doing a murder, but for pretending to be part of a conspiracy to murder?'

The Doctor looked to Marston Dawlish for help, but no help came from that quarter. I asked the next question.

'When does he get the rest of the money? On the day Commander Durden's convicted?'

'Of course not!'

'Is that your answer?' I turned to the Judge. 'My Lord, may I just remind you and the Jury, there are no large amounts of cash to be seen coming out of Commander Durden's account during the relevant period.'

With that I sat down, and counsel for the prosecution suggested that as I had taken such an unconscionable time with Doctor Wakefield, perhaps the Court would rise for the day, and he would be calling Mr Luxford in the morning.

But he didn't call the Silencer the next morning or any other morning. I don't know whether it was the news of my cross-examination in the evening paper, or a message of warning from Knuckles, but in a fit of terminal stage fright Len failed to enter the Court. A visit by the police to the house from where he carried out his window-cleaning business only revealed a distraught wife, who had no idea where he had got to. I suppose he had enough experience of the law to understand that a charge of conspiracy to murder against the Commander might turn into a charge of attempting to pervert the course of justice against Doctor Wakefield and

Len Luxford. So he went, with his cash, perhaps back to his old friends and his accustomed haunts, his one unsuccessful stab at the acting profession over.

When Marston Dawlish announced that without his vital witness the prosecution couldn't continue, Mr Justice Graves gave a heavy sigh and advised the twelve honest citizens.

'Members of the Jury, you have heard a lot of questions put by Mr Rumpole about the man – Iago. And other suggestions which may or may not have seemed to you to be relevant to this case. The simple fact of the matter is that the vital prosecution witness has gone missing – and Mr Marston Dawlish has asked me to direct you to return a verdict of "not guilty". It's an unfortunate situation, but there it is. So will your foreman please stand?'

I paid a last visit to the conference room to say goodbye to my client and Mr Crozier. The place had been cleaned up, ready to receive other sandwiches, other paper cups of coffee and other people in trouble.

'I suppose I should thank you.' The Commander was looking as confident again as he had on the telly. Only now he was smiling.

'I suppose you should thank me, the shifty old defence hack, and a couple of hard cases like Knuckles and Len Luxford. We doubtful characters saved your skin, Commander, and managed to tip the Scales of Justice in favour of the defence.'

'I shall go on protesting about that, of course.'

'I thought you might.'

'Not that I have any criticism of what you did in my case. I'm sure you acted perfectly properly. You believed in my innocence.'

'No.' I had to say it, but I'm afraid it startled him. He looked shocked. His full lips shrank in disapproval, his forehead furrowed.

'You didn't believe in my innocence?'

'My belief is suspended. It's been left hanging up in the robing room for years. It's not my job to find you innocent or guilty. That's up to the Jury. All I can do is put your case as well as you would if you had,' and I said it in all modesty, 'anything approaching my ability.'

'I don't think I'd ever have thought up your attack on the Doctor,' he admitted.

'No, I don't believe you would.'

'So I'm grateful to you.'

It wasn't an over-generous compliment, but I said thank you.

'But you say you're not convinced of my innocence?' Clearly he could hardly believe it.

'Don't worry,' I told him. 'You're free now. You can go back to work.'

'That's true. I've been suspended for far too long.' He looked at his watch as though he expected to start immediately. 'It's been an interesting experience.' I was, I must say, surprised at the imperturbable Commander, who could fall passionately in love, wish an inconvenient husband off the face of the earth and call his own criminal trial merely 'interesting'. 'We live in different worlds, Mr Rumpole,' he told me, 'you and I.'

'So we do. You believe everyone who turns up in Court is guilty. I suspect some of them may be innocent.'

'You suspect, you say, but you never know, do you?'

And so he went with Mr Crozier. I fully expect to see him again, in his impressive uniform, complaining from the television in the corner of our living-room about the Scales of Justice being constantly tipped in favour of the defence.

'I told you, Rumpole, I could tell at once that there was something fishy about that client of yours.' Hilda's verdict on the Commander was written in stone.

'But he was acquitted.'

'You know perfectly well, Rumpole, that doesn't mean a thing. The next time he turns up on the telly I shall switch over to the other channel.'

Forget Graves, I thought, leave out Bullingham; you'd search for a long time down the Old Bailey before you found a Judge as remorseless and tough as She Who Must Be Obeyed!

POCKET PENGUINS

POCKET PENGUINS